*Tink, tink, tink, tink,* sang cone-shaped jingles sewn to Grandma Wolfe's dress. Every Grandma bounce-step brought clattering *tink*s as light blurred silver against jingles of tin.

Jenna daydreamed at the kitchen table, tasting honey on fry bread, her heart beating to the *brum, brum, brum, brum* of the powwow drum.

As Moon kissed Sun good night, Jenna shifted her head on Grandma Wolfe's shoulder. "I want to jingle dance, too."

"Next powwow, you could dance Girls," Grandma Wolfe answered. "But we don't have enough time to mail-order tins for rolling jingles."

Again and again, Jenna watched a videotape of Grandma Wolfe jingle dancing. When Grandma bounce-stepped on TV, Jenna bounce-stepped on family room carpet.

But Jenna's dress would not be able to sing. It needed four rows of jingles.

As Sun fetched morning, Jenna danced east
to Great-aunt Sis's porch. Jenna's bounce-steps
crunched autumn leaves, but her steps didn't jingle.

Once again, Great-aunt Sis told Jenna a Muscogee Creek story about Bat. Although other animals had said he was too small to make a difference, Bat won a ball game by flying high and catching a ball in his teeth.

Rising sunlight reached through a windowpane and flashed against…what was it, hanging in Aunt Sis's bedroom?

Jingles on a dress too long quiet.

"May I borrow enough jingles to make a row?" Jenna asked, not wanting to take so many that Aunt Sis's dress would lose its voice.

"You may," Aunt Sis answered, rubbing her calves. "My legs don't work so good anymore. Will you dance for me?"

"I will," said Jenna with a kiss on Aunt Sis's cheek.

Now Jenna's dress needed three more rows.

As Sun arrived at midcircle, Jenna skipped south to Mrs. Scott's brand-new duplex. At Jenna's side, jingles clinked.

Mrs. Scott led Jenna into the kitchen. Once again, Jenna rolled dough, and Mrs. Scott fried it.

"May I borrow enough jingles to make a row?" Jenna asked, not wanting to take so many that Mrs. Scott's dress would lose its voice.

"You may," Mrs. Scott answered, tossing flour with her apron. "At powwow, I'll be busy selling fry bread and Indian tacos. Will you dance for me?"

"I will," said Jenna with a high five.

Now Jenna's dress needed two more rows.

As Sun caught a glimpse of Moon, Jenna strolled west to Cousin Elizabeth's apartment. At Jenna's side, jingles clanked.

Elizabeth had arrived home late from the law firm. Once again, Jenna helped Elizabeth carry in her files.

"May I borrow enough jingles to make a row?" Jenna asked, not wanting to take so many that Elizabeth's dress would lose its voice.

"You may," Elizabeth answered, burrowing through her messy closet for her jingle dress. "This weekend, I'm working on a big case and can't go to powwow. Will you dance for me?"

"I will," said Jenna, clasping her cousin's hands.

Now Jenna's dress needed one more row of jingles, but she didn't know which way to turn.

As Moon glowed pale, Jenna shuffled north to Grandma Wolfe's. At Jenna's side, jingles sat silent. High above, clouds wavered like worried ghosts.

When Jenna tugged open the door, jingles sang, *tink, tink, tink, tink.* Grandma Wolfe was jingle dancing on TV. Jenna breathed in every *hey-ah-ho-o* of a powwow song. Her heart beat *brum, brum, brum, brum* to the pounding of the drum.

On family room carpet, beaded moccasins waited for Jenna's feet. She shucked off a sneaker and slipped on a moccasin that long before had danced with Grandma Wolfe.

Jenna knew where to find her fourth row.

"May I borrow enough jingles to make a row?"
Jenna asked, not wanting to take so many that
Grandma Wolfe's dress would lose its voice.
"You may," Grandma said with a hug.
Now Jenna's dress could sing.

Every night that week, Jenna helped Grandma Wolfe sew on jingles and bring together the dance regalia.

Every night, Jenna practiced her bounce-steps.

*Brum, brum, brum, brum,* sounded the drum at
the powwow the next weekend. As light blurred
silver, Jenna jingle danced
   … for Great-aunt Sis, whose legs ached,

… for Mrs. Scott, who sold fry bread,

... for Elizabeth, who worked on her big case,

... and for Grandma Wolfe, who warmed like Sun.
*Tink, tink, tink, tink.*

## Author's Note

In this story, Jenna is a member of the Muscogee (Creek) Nation and is also of Ojibway (Chippewa/Anishinabe) descent. She lives in a contemporary intertribal community and family in Oklahoma.

Creek Nation is located in ten counties in east-central Oklahoma, and it has more than 44,000 enrolled members. The story of Bat that Great-aunt Sis retells to Jenna is a Muscogee traditional story. Ball games have been played by Native peoples for many, many generations, and stories about such games between the animals and the birds have been told by peoples of various regions of the Americas.

The home of the Ojibway people is the Great Lakes region of the United States and Canada. Ojibway women and the other Native women of Canada are often credited as the first jingle dancers, although today's graceful, dignified jingle dancers include girls and women of most Native Nations. A number of traditional stories explain the origin and purpose of the jingle dress dance, and most touch on the themes of healing and prayer.

Jingle dresses are usually made from fabric and solid in color. Hundreds of jingles are sewn directly onto the dress, or more often onto ribbons, fabric, or tape attached to the dress. These jingles are traditionally made from the silver tin or aluminum lids of snuff cans, which are rolled into cones. However, sometimes other metals are used, including gold canning lids. The jingles make a *tink, tink* noise that is often compared to rain falling on a tin roof. In the past few years, more and more dresses have incorporated fringe and ribbon work, lace, sequins, and other details.

The regalia may also include a scarf, cuffs, a bag or pouch carried in the left hand, an eagle wing or tail fan carried in the right hand, a conch or beaded belt, and boots or moccasins with leggings. Most dancers wear their hair in one braid with a feather held by a barrette or other ornament. Some dancers wear two braids to the front with barrettes.

A new dancer is a cause for joy and for her family to have a small "giveaway" to honor her. Fine gifts are given not to the person being honored but to others instead. The giveaway shows humility before the Creator, generosity, and pride in the honoree.

The number four is emphasized in Jenna's story. Many Native people believe that it is an important, even sacred, number symbolizing, for example, the four directions, four seasons, four stages of life, and four colors of man.

## Glossary

**fry bread:** a deep-fried bread often topped with honey or jam

**Indian taco:** a taco with fry bread for a base. Toppings may include chicken, turkey, duck, hamburger, elk, or venison along with grated cheddar, lettuce, tomatoes, onions, chilies, salsa, and sour cream.

**powwow:** a Native American social and spiritual event that includes dancing, drumming, singing, eating, and sometimes camping, trading, storytelling, rodeos, or film and art shows to celebrate and preserve traditions. Some are ceremonial and private in nature, while others are open to the public. Powwows are held at various times of the year, although most take place in the summer. In this story, the powwows are intertribals. Native peoples of many Nations participate in such Pan-Indian events.

**regalia:** the highly valued clothing and accessories of a dancer, not to be confused with a costume. Regalia is sometimes handed down from one generation to the next. Years are often spent bringing together the various pieces, all of which are handmade. They carry spiritual significance.